My Mother is a

CROCODILE

and other Surprises

Stories from South Africa

By Will van der Walt

Published by Ukuphuma Books

For Claudie

Table of Contents

My Mother is a Crocodile

She would be the first to deny it, of course. She sits there, in the filtered light of the bay window in the lounge, proffering the ornate teacup to her lips, as if no one on earth knows. But *I* know. And I've known for quite some time. I haven't said a word. Since yesterday, however, it's become impossible to stay mum. I saw what I saw, and though it will be difficult for others to believe, I can persuade them, because I am certain … well, as certain as one can be.

When I stop to think about it, there's that creeping doubt again: Did I really see it? Did it actually happen? When the blue-rinse ladies came for the weekly book club chat day before yesterday, I watched her welcoming them as I always do and there it was … just that hint, that something in the eye, the laugh, and the way her jaw opens when she gets enthusiastic. Then, the charm, as she shoos me off before the ladies settle in.

I go to my room and I sit there. They don't know, those ladies. They don't know what is hidden under the powdered warmth, what lurks in those hands. She turns the pages of the book under discussion with indigo nails and the much-admired opal ring … Did my father really give her that when they were courting? Or is it another subterfuge, another decoy that bobs on the dark green water, drawing an unsuspecting young swimmer ever further from the banks. How can I warn them, those ladies? How can I make them see? In the first place, they won't believe me. I'll be passed off as ill or mad or young. What saddens me is, they will have to learn the hard way. Truth will out. Since yesterday I have the evidence to cut this thing to the bone.

Or do I? Will it be regarded as evidence if I say, "I *saw* it … with my *own eyes*"? Or do they need something more? Maybe they do, but I can't keep this to myself any longer. I have known this for years and it's twisting me up. It began when I was quite small. She had beaten me for not eating my spinach and that evening when I walked past the bathroom I heard it … a distinct swishing of a tail, the sound that a crocodile makes when it thrashes about. There was no mistaking it and from that time on I have seen more and more signs.

Take the day, quite recently, when I came upon her doing her nails. She slipped the clipper away as if it had never been invented, all innocent, and that fooled me not one bit. You see, once you are aware of a thing like this, once you get wind of it, it becomes ever more difficult to hide it. The guilty party can't keep from showing its teeth, as it were. And talking of teeth, why does she want such privacy when she is in the bathroom, busy with her dental floss? That is the time when you can see it, of course, and she knows it, doesn't she just.

There are so many telling details. When she has been working in the garden, for instance, you find, next to her footprints, a kind of *trail*, something dragging on the ground behind her as she walks. What's more there are indications that she has tried to cover it up, disguise it in some way. But I can tell. When she calls me to help her, it is with that deep, guttural voice, a sound that could only come from a cavernous interior, up through a vast throat, and that she conceals very well, I must say, because she is quite a petite woman, really.

One would never suspect what she is. And clever! Let me tell you, she knows exactly how to lie below the water just with her eyes sticking out, so that no one can see the scales and claws and teeth under the sheen of the surface. But the time has come; the moment is on my shoulder. I gather my courage. I saw what I saw. It will have to be told. And damn the consequences.

I suppose what I am really up against is no one *will* believe me. I feel alone. When I tell them, though, in graphic detail, they cannot but believe me. You see, there was a matter that bothered me, even before yesterday, and now it bothers me more than ever. It is this: I am told that my brother is at boarding school and in recent weeks I have begun wondering about that. What I want to know is, when last did we have a letter, a 'phone call, anything, from him? And I won't be told, oh, that's how teenagers are, they write when they feel like it. I smell a rat, to say the least. This is probably another cover-up, you can't fool me, and when I let myself think about it for any length of time, I hear the slosh of dark water lapping about my ankles; I look carefully at the river, at any object floating by, something as innocent as a dried leaf … that's how many unfortunates have been caught: they think a twig is a twig when it's not a twig, and it's really an awesome clamp of yellowed teeth. So, I must admit, I feel uneasy about my brother, but I don't allow myself to dwell on it. It's upsetting, you know.

Then, there is the question of my sister. They say she's overseas. Now I didn't see her off at the airport and she was last in the company of my mother and, I think, my father. So I have no way of knowing whether she did leave, whether she ever arrived safely at her destination. My mother has on occasion spoken of "letters". I've never seen them. Once, apparently, there was a 'phone call, but it was on the night my father was out, playing poker, and I myself was already in bed. I didn't hear any telephone ringing. So the question remains, was there in fact a 'phone call? But, more disquieting, is my sister really in another country?

It's agony living with this, but I'm happy to say - if one can be happy in such matters - that my agony will soon be over, that is, when I finally reveal it all. They'll be horrified, I know. I'll have to find ways of breaking it gently. But would be possible, though? I mean, the only gentle thing here is my mother's exterior, her benign gaze, the engaging smile. And the Voice which enchants everyone ... deep and, as they say, thee-ahtrical, expressive, well intoned, articulate in pronouncements. Behind all of that, of course, there is the Truth, the truth that ripples along in the opaque shallows, past the reeds, never seen for the horror it is, the armoured skin, the powerful claws... And the Teeth ... that jaundiced, jagged line, mountainously irregular, opening up, widening in silent laughter.

So, as I say, it will take courage, all the strength. I have to believe that I can do it. Perhaps it's a mission, a kind of crusade, exposing what needs to be exposed.

They probably won't return, those blue-rinse ladies, once they know. Other members of the family, the neighbours … how will they take it? I can't say, but I must not be deterred. I can't flinch. The truth hurts, but it will hurt even more if I don't do this. Now, let me calmly review the details.

I came home yesterday a little earlier than usual. I didn't hear anything on entry. There might have been a grunt or a gasp from the lounge, but I can't be sure. I went up to my room, put my tennis racket down. Then I heard it … a slurp. That's the only way to describe it. It was as if lips were being smacked. Fear gripped me. Was my father home? I don't remember having seen his car in the driveway.

I stood at the top of the stairs and I listened. The lounge door was slightly ajar. The house was silent. I ventured down a step or two, straining for any tell-tale sound. Then I heard something. It might have been a creak on the staircase, I don't know, but I rather imagine that it was the kind of noise one hears when the throat is wide open, what one hears at a dentist's, when the teeth are in huge array.

With my hand on the banister I came down the stairs, my eyes fixed on the lounge door. All was quiet now.

What was going on in that room? The antique furniture, the vases, the paintings, curtains … what were they witnessing?

I didn't knock, some instinct told me not to. I put my hand on the door, pushing a little. On the mantlepiece I could see the goldfish bowl. It was empty. By degrees, the edge of the door revealed ever more of the room.

But before the whole of the lounge came into view, I heard what could only be described as a gurgle, a sort of struggle … and then I saw my mother at the bay window, her back slightly to me and she was patting her lips, breaking a little burp discretely, as if she had just swallowed a mouthful, and I could have sworn she was tucking something into her lips. Something spaghetti-like. Was it a shoelace?

"Oh!" she said, acting surprised when she saw me. "Don't sneak up on me like that! My nerves!"

Her nerves… My eye!

"Where is my father?" I demanded.

"Your father?" she said, casting her eyes down. She was playing for time.

"You know exactly what I'm talking about, Mother." I thought of the shoelace.

"Don't be silly," she said. "Your father is on a business trip. He won't be back for a week, maybe two or three weeks, I'm not sure. He 'phoned last night, after you'd gone to bed."

You've eaten him, I thought. You've devoured him, and you won't admit it.

"Why are you … you staring at me like that, darling? Why don't you … sit down? Come, next to me, and have a bit of *jaw* with your old mother. *"*

She stretched out her hand. I stepped back. Her eyes glittered. The room tilted like a see-saw. The roof turned. Everything cascaded through the air … a tsunami of paintings, carpets, chairs, fish tank, footstool, coffee table… everything falls into that yawning canyon of a jaw, sinks down to the flesh warm innards of the great earth.

I sighed. I'll get nothing out of you now, I thought, whatever is *in* you. It's all too deep. But *this* time I *saw* it… with my own eyes.

"Never *mind*," I said, turned on my heel, went out of the lounge, up the stairs and into my room. Never mind, I thought, I won't get anything out of you now, mother … your lips are sealed, so to speak, clamped shut. But there's no escaping it. I have what I need to tell the world.

Then again, who will believe me? Certainly not the blue-rinse ladies. Perhaps I need to wait a bit, until my father "gets back", if you know what I mean. But for myself, I'll have to be very watchful indeed.

§§§

Melani

Melani was a man. I say *was* not because she is dead now since, in one sense, she was never alive. I say *was* because Melvyn made her. Now here again, it is easy for me to be misunderstood. Melvyn is not a promoter of ravishing models throwing their hips as they flow down the catwalk, looking through people with unsmiling deadpan. He is not one to pop champagne over a million dollar contract in an all-window office overlooking the New York cityscape with this living, breathing magnificence by his side. No, none of that. Melvyn is a suburban, moving and thinking in a cluttered room where his computer monitor and tower stand like Assyrian gods, proud and beige.

Talking of gods, Melvyn was a bit like one in his making of Melani. She was his creation. He fashioned her, not from coffee-coloured clay, but from a photograph he saw in a magazine at the doctors' rooms and which he sneakily tore out. He breathed life into her with his mind, with the tips of fingers dancing, like a devil, on the computer keys. Each client on Compu-Date has a profile ("Why you should get to know me") and hers was one of fire and ice. "I was a Bengal tigress in a last incarnation, now, an independent one, with razor-sharp claws. I eat stupid men alive, then spit out the fur, bones and gonads."

In the temperate valley of her thigh lies a whip.

"I use my silky long hair and slender tongue to massage your rock-hard six pack".

Cloistered in cyber space, she was Salome, Jezebel and Mata Hari. Like Vishnu, she had a healing hand and a destructive one. Her full lips breathed *Come hither, but hie thee hence!* An orgasm behind steel and stone. She defined svelte. A longish face with a canny glint in the sidelong glance, a butter blonde that might even have been a feminine man, with all the intrigue of the androgyne. Too intelligent, too daring to be sultry, her eyes were shafts of knowing, the erotic promise skilfully mascara'd.

And the e-mails poured in.

Within seven days of Melvyn crafting the profile she was the sixth most sought after woman on Compu-Date. Within 14 days Melvyn noted that her profile had been visited by over a thousand men. There were too, 87 women who, it seemed, were hopeful that Melani might have overlooked some proclivity for her own gender.

And the men panted.

They laid their BMW's, their MG's at her feet, their yachts, their mansions, their suave portraits, flamboyant promises of love, glittering futures, travel to distant places. They wavered though, before the towering intellect they faced. "Men who have not read Fritz Perls, Dostoyefski, Nietzsche, Schopenhauer, Sartre, Joyce, Goethe and Spike Milligan need not apply." All they could do was to throw compensations at the lady.

And Melvyn worked.

Dismissals came thick, fast and furious. Dozens of e-mails stabbed disappointed hearts. It was a massacre. Hopes died like flies. New victims paraded themselves. The inbox was dark with bold-font replies.

Then the international interest began.

A Brazilian coffee magnate offered her a penthouse in the Copacabana, threatening to zoom in and scoop her up in his private jet.

A diamond seller from Novgorod, rumoured to own "half of St Petersburg", lifted his Russian heart into her hands.

Three well-known movie-makers in LA unconditionally offered Melani main roles in big-budget movies. No auditions needed.

One evening idly deleting one e-mail after another, an exhausted Melvyn came across a reply that caught his eye. He read and re-read it. Then he printed it out. And stared at it.

Dear Melani

I read your profile and felt deeply drawn to you. I don't have much to offer you in the line of possessions, but, looking at your reading list, I take the liberty of mentioning that I did my Ph.D. on Jean-Paul Sartre – "The Prolegomena of Reversible Ambiguities in Sartre's 'Being and Nothingness', with special reference to ontic bi-camerality".

I can't offer you a relationship as much as I would love that. I offer myself as a friend.

I have recently been diagnosed as having a malignant brain tumour and have four months to live. I would like you to be my friend in that time.

Yours

David du Toit

The paper rustled in Melvyn's hand. His eyes ached and something was burning in his nose. Then he went online.

Dear David
My name is Melvyn Sullivan. I have told you and
others a lie. Melani does not exist. I created her.
I am truly sorry to have done this to you.
I offer my friendship instead.

Then Melvyn committed murder. Not the dripping axe, gothic type. The deed was clicks on a keyboard and a clean terminal finger hitting the *delete* button. Melani was dead. She evaporated into the sunless vaults of cyber space.

The photograph was burnt and its ashes scattered on a tidal rock in Table Bay.

Perhaps all of this was saying that Melvyn was not so much a god of love, but a god of irony, playing with frailties - the Hindus call it *Lila*, the sport of gods. Men and some women had clambered needily, pressing their noses of longing against the pane of their monitors, debarred from a fugitive beauty that probably haunts us all.

I don't know whether David du Toit ever accepted Melvyn's offer of friendship. I didn't ask.

§§§

Flight

An itch, then the eyes began to flicker. Above him, some lunatic thing … the broken elbow of a wing above the cockpit of the F-14. Somewhere in him there was a siren rising. Thoughts shot through him like tracer bullets. It was already daylight. He must have been unconscious for at least two hours. Was he hurt? He opened and closed his fist in the gloves. He leant forward, thinking of his back, moved his toes in the boots. Relief glowed in him. He turned his head left, right, there was pain. Must have been a whiplash when the 'plane came down. Something was tickling his cheek. Blood. A cut.

He had to get out, it was day. Before the Enemy he was defenceless. The hatch was stuck. He pitched in all his reserve strength, pushed with gritted teeth, until the hatch rattled, moved and slid open. He took his helmet off and lifted himself out of the cockpit into the morning air.

All around him there was a barren landscape. His headache came in waves. A silence hung over everything. In the distance he could see black mountain ridges. I must be somewhere south of the city of Karbala, he thought. He had seen the dry lake of Wadi al Milh from the air. I must be about 30 to 50 kilometres from there, difficult to say. But I am alive, thank God for that.

He lifted himself out completely, felt dizzy for a moment. When it cleared, he peered down and examined the fuselage of the F-14. The 'plane was crushed onto a rock outcrop. He sighed and looked at the landscape again. He must be plus-minus 100 kilometres from the Saudi border. Base will come looking for me, he thought, I can count on that. Apache helicopters picked up five guys during the raid the night before. Snatched from the jaws of the Enemy. But it's no comfort: I flew off course last night.

He clambered down and jumped onto the ground. He looked up at the 'plane, still dizzy with the thought that there was blood flowing through his veins.

His watch was working. It was 7:15. He had last looked at his watch at five o'clock that morning. Enemy must know that I was hit and they'll be on their way, make no mistake. Images moved into his mind: prisoners had been taken, paraded before the world television channels … broken, bruised faces hanging between cowed shoulders. The pilots at base had become quiet. Who knows what those guys have gone through? someone said. If they're still alive. War's a bastard.

He had to hurry, to get onto high ground so that the Apaches could spot him. Karbala lay more or less that way, Baghdad to the north-east. Enemy could pinpoint his position, were probably sending a truckful of soldiers at this very moment. It would take them two to three hours.

With shooting pains in his neck, he climbed up the rocks. At the top he looked north-east. Something caught his eye. A dust cloud. Which could mean only one thing. A vehicle.

It was like a blow in the guts. He slid down the rocks, made for the cockpit. They were on the way. All he could do was to flee. Pistol, ammunition, the water bottle, map. That vehicle is probably 15 to 20 kilometres away. My I.D. documents I've got. Leave the helmet and take a floppy hat.

Within three-quarters of an hour Enemy's combat boots stride about this wreck, he thought. Suddenly he heard the strange language, the aha's, the dark satisfaction. He saw the swarthy faces with heavy moustaches, how they savoured their hatred. He snatched the compass, unscrewed the flare gun, clipped it onto his belt, took two, three flares, slipped the pack of vitamins into his pocket. Three days' supply.

With a sting of despair, he glanced up at the sky, straining to hear the blades of the Apaches. He looked again in the direction of the dust cloud, but saw nothing. It was deceptive. Dust could easily be hidden by a hollow. His courage was ebbing. More than a 100 kilometres from the border, he thought, with swarms of soldiers, landmines, watchtowers, enemy 'planes and helicopters. Was there any chance? If I stay...

No, he thought, jumping down onto the ground. Enemy isn't taking prisoners, not out here in the desert. Will they put bullets through my kneecaps and leave me to die?

He became conscious that he was jogging. There was no wind and his footprints lay like invitations. He took a last glance at the F-14, crumpled against the rock, as if that wreck could in some way comfort him. It was the last familiar thing he would see. How far could he get before the moaning engines of the trucks broke this massive silence? Before he heard the voices?

Where are the Apaches? The thundering blades, the strong hands hauling me into the cockpit, the manly embrace. Oh my God, where are they? Feel helpless, naked like a child. Hands, save me now.

Right, just keep the running rhythmic, not too fast, not too slow. Look back. Can't see the ridge where the F-14 is any more. They can cover this distance to me in 15 minutes. Just move along the rock surfaces. More difficult, but it leaves no footprints. They'll be here, all right. Time is everything now. Keep the rhythm, not too fast, not too slow.

Compass says south lies this way, straight ahead. This treeless landscape, this silence... Wait for a moment, catch my breath. There's a ridge on the horizon, must be five k's from here. Take some water. Not too much. I'll make for that ridge. Wipe the mouth. Move on.

There is a small farmhouse in a nook of trees in the gentle rolling hills of Maryland. A white walled silo. Cattle grazing. The gushing of water in the reservoir. A father calling under a cloud-raked sky.

Three hours have passed. I'm probably 20 to 25 kilometres from the 'plane. And all about me this world of no sound... a silence that seeps into you like a liquid and lies at the back of your brain, rises, moves around in the skull, sinks through the spine, into the fibres, into the hands and legs. It touches the forehead with ceremony, like a God ritual.

I feel strange. Headache gone. My neck pain has disappeared. I can't see the dust cloud anymore. A pale sky and a mild sun.

This flare gun. Undo it. Probably just give me away, when I use it. Enemy will easily spot a flare in the night sky. A dull thud and the flare gun lies in the sand. Let me move on.

A few trees. Rocks with strange wind carved hollows. Let me get this flying jacket off, hang it over my shoulder as I walk. The compass is acting up a bit, may be a magnetic region. More strange hollows in the rocks, these red formations with their hollows like ghosts.

The rocks are thinning out. The land is beginning to slope slightly. Shadows are getting longer. Late afternoon. This plain too, has no grass and no trees. The evening will be cooler.

The stars of the night hang low. My footfalls are a light crunch on the soil. They make a rhythm. These footfalls in this dark are those of the last man on earth. So it feels. I have left the noise of soldiers and sirens behind, tarmacs and propellers, greasy hands and blood.

Did they ever exist? Is the noise of war not merely a wisp of thought in the midst of vast silence?

In the morning light, the ground is dewed. Stones glisten. At noon, the flying jacket falls to the sand. In the afternoon, the pistol and the ammunition. When the stars spread out the night again, the map lies deserted on a rock.

There is grass when the sun rises. There are trees and fresh water that makes rocks shine. For the first time, the dried blood may be washed from the cheek. Birds clap their wings on the ridge of a rise. The shirt and hat hang on a dry branch. The I.D. book lies in the grass.

Midday the watch falls on hard ground. At midnight, the compass. In the windless dawn the boots stand by an old tree stump, the socks a little further. When the sun is high, the trousers crumple to stones.

At midnight I stand naked on the high ridge. I breathe deeply. I feel the silence against my face and let it into me. It seeps deeply. Then direction fills me and I move down from the ridge. Light begins to fill the world, the sun rises. I walk into the morning, the warmth on my shoulders, my knees, my penis, my arms, my back, my elbows, my buttocks, my feet, my face. I enter the plain and grow small in the distance.

* * * * * *

Years after the first Gulf War there has arisen
amongst the nomads of the southern deserts a story of a
man healing sickness. He lives in the Ruins of Al
Machmi, they say, and they have a name for him. The
man is called He who Sings to the Dustwinds on the Plain
of Ghosts. He cannot speak the language of the region
and heals only in silence. He is seldom seen. A French
archaeologist, who has devoted a lifetime of study to the
mysterious origins and meaning of the Ruins, has
evidently met him. The man has blond hair and an ugly
scar on his left cheek.

§§§

Spinach

She pushed aside the little dark mound on her plate and declared with a pout that she didn't want it, she wasn't going to eat it because it wasn't nice. Maggie didn't force her. There's no sense in compelling a child to eat food, if she doesn't want it.

I thought, How different things are! I ate my spinach, because Maggie has a wonderful cheese sauce that goes with it, and, of course, the garlic, which is the cherry on top, so to speak. But my mind was alive with memory.

I watched Tammy eating her peas and pumpkin, but the spinach lay untouched.

My own plate was an expanse of emptiness. I had eaten what had been put before me.

"Because once you start with that … " I heard my mother say as the memory grew, "once you let a child say, `I don't want this. I don't want that …' That's when you're looking for trouble." My father took her up on that. On the nights she made spinach for us, I could feel him watching my plate, watching me. And I watched my mother dish up the dark strings of spinach that I knew had boiled and boiled in the kitchen and were close to uneatable. She wasn't a cook, my mother. My sisters have proved better cooks than she. Her asthma or something kept her from standing in the steam by the stove. With the spinach, she had simply let the boiling water do it for her.

So my father watched me. I ate the carrots. I ate the mashed potato. I ate the boerewors.

I cut the spinach. I tried to cut it. It was tough. I managed to get some of the strings - it looked like drowned hair - managed to get it onto my fork. And then, into my mouth. I chewed. I chewed. My teeth couldn't get the stuff crushed in my mouth. I tried to swallow it. I couldn't. Got some down. The rest was too daunting. I'd leave it. And it lay there, open for all to see. Once, - I think I'd just turned eight - I pushed it into a line, and then with a quick sidelong glance, lay my knife and fork over it, so that it couldn't be seen. It didn't work.

"Eat your spinach … " said my father.

It was not so much an order, as an early warning, because we had been through this before. I don't know why, but it was becoming increasingly difficult to eat spinach.

"But I … "

"*You eat it.*" The warning was now edging toward an ultimatum. Well I knew what lay beyond that. There was a reasonableness in that voice, a conviction that once you allow a child to leave food on its plate, you start the slippery slide towards spoiling the child. The next thing is, the child starts telling *you* where to get off. No. No. You can't allow that; it's not the way to rear a child. They must eat what's put before them.

"You eat that food or I take you to the room."

There's some rat or dusty rodent blocking my throat and when I force the dark stuff into my mouth, I can feel the gorge rising … the rat is forcing it up. I can't swallow these strings, tough hair.

"You don't want to listen … "

The spinach lies before me on the white snowscape of the plate, a smear, a pile, a stain, a labyrinth, a destiny. I want to flee, disappear between the potato tureen and the bowl of carrots, off the table out of the door and liberate myself into the evening air beyond the verandah.

Then the scrape of the chair as my father gets to his feet, a sound easily as frightening as the screech of tyres.

A gale of crying bursts from me as my father's strong hand clamps down on me, drags me from the table, down the passage into the room. My howling anticipates the strap blows to my legs, then it's not anticipation anymore, it's the real thing. But somehow the anticipation helps to numb the hitting.

He would beat me with a rhythm, punctuate the blows with "How … many … times … have … I … " as if he were knocking a nail of moral worth into me and I would be a well-adjusted construct when he had done with me, and I would no longer resist the values that had been handed down to him - by his father's hand. But it wasn't the values. I swear it wasn't the values. It was just that spinach.

Then he left me. I was dripping humiliation, aflame with stinging legs.

I hadn't said anything about the spinach, hadn't even tried to insert between the blows the words that would make my father pause, frown, and thoughtfully hang the strap up behind the door again. It is something you can't explain to a father. That unswerving purpose could move the Pyramids of Egypt. Remonstrances about the impalatability of the spinach were beyond my nine-year-old capacity. I couldn't do it.

I went back down the passage, shut up my ragged breathing and took up my place at the table again where my mother was still sitting, her demure mien a badge of confident knowing. She was certain that however awful that might have sounded, it was for the best. Because once you start *that* …

I've understood that my father took my difficulty with the spinach personally. Somehow I was trying to insult my mother. Somehow I was being maliciously stubborn, a snide perversity in not eating that spinach. And once you start - You see, the way youth is going... My father had to protect my mother because, after all, she had slaved for hours over a hot stove to prepare this meal and here was I, little ingrate, pulling up my nose at what she put before me. You can see how it goes: It starts with the little things, next it's food and then going out at night, smoking and drinking, and ever-increasing lawlessness. And if you don't look out...

I sit down. Before me, the spinach, a dark prominence of igneous rock silent in a white-sand desert. I pick up the knife. I pick up the fork. I approach. I cut the spinach, cold now, saw through the cold strands, saw with flying elbows as best I can. (Is this flaming knife blunt?) I get the stuff onto my fork, get it to stay there. If my father isn't looking, he's listening for the faintest wisp of protest. Then I lift it to my mouth, force it in, down my narrow throat, a tunnel that's closing in by the second, the cold spinach, against the lurking rat … I'm going to throw this mush up again … Please, don't … dust-ridden unfeeling rodent … I manage to swallow the first mouthful.

I fetched Maggie some more wine and refilled my glass at the same time. We listened to Tammy telling about something that had happened at school. Maggie and I would be married in a month or two. My uncertainties about my new role as a step-father to Tammy had compounded when one evening she had with certain perversity hit my backside as I'd bent to pick up something. It could have been that she was testing her young power; it could be that I was seen to be monopolising her mother's affections. I had reacted badly. I had stood up and wagging a deadly serious finger at her, told her that if ever she did anything like that again I would give her a hiding she wouldn't forget. In the same instant, a desperation came over me. I had hated the violence visited on me as a nine-year-old, as a seven-year-old, ten-year-old, eight-year-old, eleven. How could I ever do that? I had made an appointment at the Parents Centre for advice in step-parenting. "Yes," the counsellor said, "you haven't been a father and in the middle-years it's difficult to make the adjustment."

Maggie thanked me for the wine and then, with routine sternness, told Tammy it was her bath-time and that there was school tomorrow. Rebellion came and went like a breeze. Then the girl got up and went down the passage.

I looked at Tammy's plate on the table and told the story of my childhood. Maggie told me that her parents had never been strict about food. About other things, yes, but not food. We chatted a little about arrangements for the wedding, the guest list, reception. And we mustn't forget to give Michael a call about the service. Then I gathered my plate and Tammy's. Maggie brought her own, came with me to the kitchen.

The light bulb had blown earlier on and the kitchen was in semi-darkness with light coming in from the passage. Maggie put down her plate. I set down my plate and Tammy's.

"Are you still going to work tonight?" she asked, laying a hand on mine.

"No, love, I'll just give these plates a once-over and I'll join you."

"You know, that child hasn't run her bath yet." She sighed. "I'll have to go and sort her out. Don't be long." She moved off into the light of the passage.

In the half light I washed my plate and was about to scrape the spinach from Tammy's into the rubbish-bin when I stopped. It was cold by now, that spinach, the little dark mound. But I found myself taking a fork and slipping it into the cheese-dolloped spinach, catching the garlic again, I popped it into my mouth, deliciously, and, savouring the texture, I finished it off.

§§§

The Black Glove

Arnie didn't buy everything that Bess believed after she went religious. But he wasn't under any pressure, as far as I could see. Her particular brand of faith was inward. Her eyes softened and her smile remained what it had always been, the way I had known her since we were small. After her diagnosis I would watch her watering the poinsettias and sitting awhile with St Francis, a figurine she had brought back with her from Assisi when she and Arnie had been to Europe.

My cynicism about religion took a bit of a battering, precisely because there was no righteousness in my sister, seat-reserved-in-heaven stuff. She had only gentle advice when I had been involved in the juvenile court as a teenager. After my destructive marriage with Norma – six years of turmoil – she said, Stay with us, our granny flat is empty now. I did. She had never judged me when I had unpacked my woes. She had listened. She was not that changed when she went religious. She was already perfect, I thought wryly.

You and Arnie get on, she said before I moved in and it was true. They had no children and Arnie was to become a mentor to me. I had never had such a friend.

He and I would retire to the lounge, he in the armchair and I on the sofa with a bottle of port between us. On occasion Bess joined us and we matched our differences, never with any better-than's. It had a most calming effect as she outlined, at the pause of a discussion, where our ideas diverged.

The topics were, of course, profound – Have atheists composed any great choral music? Is religion born in the fear of death? Can the "conservation of energy" phenomenon be equated with the soul? And discussion would not stop until the flagon of port was empty. "When we start talking nonsense." Arnie grimaced with a twinkle.

Living there I was witness to their relationship. If you can be sceptical about things you can't see, you struggle with the ones you can. I was looking at perfection. They had a lovely balance between raunchiness and intellectual sharing. There was a lot of tart banter over the kitchen sink. They would sit side by side at the computer flipping through their photographs and memories from Europe with abandon. They would return clean and serene from a weekend at the hotwater spa. They fought and it lasted for all of a minute or two. He or she would declare, "Oh hell, I hate fighting. Let's stop" and they would. Even with a giggle. Their childlessness seemed to draw them closer. So did her diagnosis.

I was present when Arnie told Flora what the doctor had said. The old woman's eyes searched the floor for something that was not there. From now on, Arnie said, Bess would not be able to help her with the house as she had done in the past. Flora was affected. She had known Bess since she was a little girl.

Our discussions became fewer. He spent most of his after-dinner time with Bess. One evening he came down from the bedroom and said to me, "She wants to pray or something". He glanced up the stairs.

"Oh," I said, fitting a short log into the flames in the hearth. I saw that he was fetching a bottle of port.

We nursed our drinks in silence for a while. When he spoke, he sounded tired. "She … " He stared at the surface of the port in his glass with a frown. "She doesn't have very much longer, Den."

I knew this. Bess had told me herself and without any theatrics. Serene as only she could be.

"I don't know … " He leaned forward as if in pain. "I don't know what I'm going to do without her."

"Yes," I sighed, wanting to add "It won't be easy" but I didn't. Bess would be my loss as well. I had loved her as I have loved no-one else. To think of the passage, the stairs, the garden, their bedroom - my own life - without her. It was as if a soundless siren swelled and sank in me for some seconds.

He sipped at his port, examined the rim of the glass. "She said she won't leave me."

I looked at him.

"She says, she refuses to live without me. She says she'll be here. She says God will allow it."

I drained my glass, not knowing what to comment, careful not to say anything that would betray my irritation. I thought, Don't get lost in your own views here. Support this man.

"How ..." I measured my words. " ... will you know, Arnie?" Perhaps what I was saying would bring him back to earth.

"She said ..." He pouted. "She said she'd leave a sign that she's here or if she isn't here then she's still ... that she ... well, loves me, I suppose."

"Leave a sign," I murmured, not knowing what else to say.

"You know those black gloves that your mother left her?"

"The opera gloves?"

"She'll put one of them on her dresser, you know, once she's ..." He was searching for words. " ... on the other, you know, the other side"

There was no irony in him. He seemed to believe what he was saying. All the razor-sharp comment, the insights, the muscular reasoning, all that he and I had shared at that fireside, all was gone now. I was looking at a man already deep in grief and attempting to comfort himself even if it meant tossing aside what he stood for. What could I say?

"I saw a movie like that once," I said, feeling helpless. "Could've been a book I read." This is not the time to argue with Arnie. Leave him. Let him be. We didn't finish the port.

My sister's funeral was a quiet one. Arnie requested that there be no music and afterward we went to Peggy and John's for coffee and scones. I drove Arnie home in silence.

Arnie removed his things from the bedroom and put them in the guest suite where he now slept. He locked their bedroom and kept the key. Flora would bring us supper at night and he might sit a while before going to bed. There were no more discussions. I went off to the granny flat attending to my own grief, knowing somehow that his pain was deeper than mine. I had to help this man as I could. I understood that he was the father I had never had.

I knew that for most people the real grieving only begins after some period, a month or so. I bided my time, noticing that he would sometimes go into the room and sit at the foot of the bed. He wasn't secretive about it. He told me he needed to do this.

One evening I heard him coughing upstairs and when it persisted I went up the stairs to find him in the bathroom staring at the facecloth in his hands. It had blood on. I bundled him into the car and rushed to the hospital where he was admitted.

He went back to work after a week, but he wasn't looking well. There were more tests and he had to take a handful of pills each morning.

One afternoon while he was at work I asked Flora for her key to the bedroom, a key that Arnie did not know about. I unlocked the door and entered, half expected to see Bess propped up with pillows watching a movie on her laptop. The sense of her presence was strong. I opened her cupboard and going through three or four drawers, I found the black gloves. I took one out and laid it across the dresser top where some of her make-up still stood. I left the room, locked and returned the key to Flora. I said nothing to her about the glove and asked her not say that she had a key and that I had asked for it. I told her it was important for his grieving that he did not know about this key. She looked puzzled but seemed to accept what I said. I added God is OK with some lies we tell. It made me feel funny to say it.

At five Arnie came in the front door in a coughing fit and had to sit down for a while as I fetched him syrup to still the convulsion. I brought a glass of water as well. He looked pallid.

He didn't eat much of Flora's supper and went straight upstairs. I sat down on the settee.

I wondered whether he would go into the bedroom. Why had I done it? I was trying to help him, I told myself. But how do you help someone if you know what you're doing is wrong, if it is a lie? But was it a lie? Hadn't I felt Bess's presence in that room? Was Bess beckoning to me from across the divide? saying, Here you are, put this glove across the dresser so that dearest

Arnie knows I'm fine. It had been my hand, but it was her spirit.

Stop this necromantic drivel! my mind shouted. Your grief is doing this to you. Was there any port …?

I heard Arnie coming down the stairs. I heard him stop. I turned to see him standing with one hand on the banister. He slowly came up to his chair. In his other hand I saw the glove. He sat down.

"She's … " The glove lay in his hand. "She's been here, Den."

"I'm … glad", I said. I was now feeling like Judas.

"She left the glove as she said she would."

"Does that mean …" I was forcing myself to say something.

"It means she's been here." He was staring out into the room.

Think quickly, I told myself. You're in this up to your ears. "It means she loves you, Arnie."

"I've never doubted that, Den." He turned to me for the first time.

Would my action send him over the edge? What a stupid thing to have done! What was I thinking of? What an infernal, irresponsible thing to do!

We sat in silence for some minutes and then Arnie got up. "I think there's some port left," he said.

In the weeks and months that followed I came to stand before the realization that Arnie was willing himself to death. The mind is a powerful thing and it was probably because he could not bear to be alone any more. She was on the other side and he could not touch her. I took him hiking but we had to turn back halfway. The weekend to the spa was a little better though I knew it was memory-laden for him. The week after that he went for another examination and the doctor took me aside and said that he thought Arnie was deeply depressed. This was affecting him.

"He told me something different," Arnie said handing me my port from his chair. "Particularly after I told him I wasn't that interested in reaching my sixtieth birthday next May."

"What did he say?" I sipped the port.

"He said you don't help your own healing with that attitude." He turned to me with a broad grin. "I'm going, Den."

"Oh, come on, Arnie," I said. "You've got a lot of kick in you and Bess would've wanted you to ..."

"No, Den," he interrupted. "Don't go there. She wants me. And, to be perfectly candid, I'm ready to go." He topped up my glass.

I sat, gloomy about his words. You can't answer this. He has to speak.

"And, Den ..."

It was the approach of jollity in his tone that made me look up.

He raised his brows, his hand poised with the port glass. "I'll let you know. When I'm - you know - on the other side."

What had I started with my foolish act?

Arnie's health sank steadily after that. About a month later I had to find a nurse who would look after him at home. I sat by his bed, but he didn't always feel like company. His colleagues came to see him and his boss popped in for a few visits.

Flora was most dependable and even steadied me in my darker moments alone at the supper table. Now the bedroom door stood open. Flora would take tea to Arnie and they had chats. He might have been preparing her for what was to come.

Eleven months after Bess had been buried, Arnie himself died. The doctors agreed that a "severe depression" must have contributed. I knew they were wrong. After the funeral there was coffee and scones at Peggy and John's and I drove home.

At supper I told Flora "just to go", I would tidy up the kitchen. She said, "Mr Arnie told me to look after you." Her old eyes fixed me for a moment. I said thank you curtly and ushered her out of the kitchen and locked the door. I saw my food in a plate in the oven. I took it out and smashed it on the floor. And shouted and went into the lounge and flopped onto the settee and got up and fetched a bottle of port from the liquor cabinet and opened it and drank most of it.

I was blind angry with a world that kept alive the myth that life continues after death, that there's a thing called heaven where everything is hunkey dory, that people are duped into all of this from their childhood. I hated myself for being part of it, for fooling Arnie into believing that my sister Bess, his dearly loved wife, had been back to this house, visiting us from the other side. I hated myself for it all. I was angry that the myth was not true. I wanted it to be true.

Let me sleep, I thought. Let me go to my granny flat and sleep because oblivion is the only meaning there is.

The room tilted a little but I walked, with determination, out of that lounge.

I flopped onto my bed, knowing that the sickness rising in me was not only the liquor. I was drawing the hard breath of a drunk man. I thought, Get into your pyjamas and sleep and sleep. Oblivion is the ...

I reached for my bedside lamp in the darkness.

There was something soft across the switch and even before I pressed the switch to light up what was now in my hand I knew what it was.

Through the stupor I smiled. Arnie, you bugger, I thought, you've been here. It was Flora's hand, I know. But you put it there.

§§§

Understanding Glass

When I got into my car that morning, there was a bee hovering on the inside against the windscreen. I put my sandwiches on the passenger seat. With any other kind of insect, you don't hesitate - a ruthless ball of thumb or the side of a fist, which settles the problem in a blink. With a bee, of course, it's different.

It must have slipped in the previous afternoon when I came home, parking as I do, in the driveway. I guardedly reached over, keeping close tabs on what the thing was doing, half expecting it to fly into my face on a kamikaze mission. I rolled down the passenger window so that the damn' thing could get out. I don't like bees. My father died from bee stings. He had been a sick man admittedly, but I still don't like bees. I glanced at my watch and drove off with it fussily buzzing, hunched against the windscreen, trying to drill its way through the glass.

There's a stop sign ahead, I thought. Maybe I can take my packet of sandwiches and crush the creature against the glass, but then you never know: if you're not successful and you think you've done the deed, you lift the sandwiches (which are now a mess) and you've got an angry bee on your hands, on your arms, on your forehead.

I watched from the corner of my eye, turned into the boulevard, watching ... I stopped at the traffic lights. Me and the bee, we stopped, except that he didn't stop; he was in perpetual motion, his own quiet desperation burning against the glass. I was a little ahead of the bumper-to-bumper commuting that I had become accustomed to since moving to this suburb. I was early because there had been no fond farewell between Maggie and me. In fact, if you said our knives were out for each other, I would say machetes, more like it. We had slept separately the previous night as had also happened in the early weeks of our marriage a few months before. The adjustment at our age, I am told, is that much greater. Our knives were out or was it only *my* knife?

The stupid bee was still bumping up against the glass. I glanced at it as a green-arrowed light urged the direction to the freeway. I negotiated my place in the flow of cars, trucks, minibuses. Idiotic thing ... Whatever multi-vision these insects have it is still tunnel vision if it cannot see that, behind it, there is a huge open window, a gap fifty, sixty, hundred times its own size and letting in a nippy little breeze, I noticed. If it couldn't see the window, why couldn't it *sense* the way out? I wondered for a moment how many eyes a bee had. Ears ... couldn't it *hear* the mighty rush at its back?

I was tired. I was irritable. I'd slept very little. Tossed and turned and was turbulent. Well, turbulent, not really, but a certain churning, a half-conscious rehearsing of arguments in my mind with Maggie who was in the lounge, smoking one cigarette after the other. We were working hard on our relationship, trying to. We had read a book on the ways men and women interact, but it hadn't helped us, not in this, the latest round of fights. The book did speak to us, I admit. It made good sense. In our calm moments we understood our differences, could recite the theories. But the depth of bitterness in our exchanges, the gall of it, was disturbing.

The bee was murmuring its way towards my side of the windscreen, menace in that sound which reminded me of a distant circular saw. The insanity of the kamikaze culture - a being destroying itself to make a point: you anger me, pal, and yes, I'll die defending myself, but you won't get off lightly and you won't forget me. My death will serve the posterity of bees. I'll build a little monument on your hand, your arm, your forehead.

I should have crushed the blasted thing with my packet of sandwiches, but I couldn't do that now. It was too late. The traffic was not dependable. At any moment there could be a slowing up ahead and then, with shock, you see that the car in front of you is closer than you gauged, closing in fast. Anyway, the traffic was in fact cruising along quite nicely, fairly open at this time of the day. At this point, the bee which hadn't actually left the windscreen, started bouncing in ever-widening bounces, abseiling, ropeless, from that inexplicable transparent cliff-face that was and wasn't there. It was not as yet interested in what the inner depths the car might hold, despite the fact that the window …

It continued to probe and prod at the glass. Just stay away from my face, I thought. And my throat.

It knocked ceaselessly, blindly, uncomprehendingly against the windscreen, over and over again. Above the passenger seat the open window gaped a windswept gateway to freedom.

My mind was dull. I had funny thoughts. I suppose, I mused, a bee can't see how glass functions. I mean, there is this whole world beyond the windscreen, a landscape filled with an early morning vista of a grainy Table Mountain, its crags and shadows fresh and sharp, and yet you, dear bee, can't get to it.

Glass … funny stuff. For no reason I remembered playing with shard of broken glass as a child. My mother saw this, prised it from my young sweaty fingers, saying, Don't play with glass; it'll cut you. Silly, I thought, when she left: you cut yourself with *knives*. Knives are sharp things, *that* I know. Not glass. I got up, located the shard where she'd put it and I looked at it. I picked it up, rubbed my thumb hard on its clean edge, sceptical until it sank deep into the flesh, my finger suddenly a blossom of blood, an itch of pain welling up in the ball of my thumb. It seemed strange - it still seems strange - that something you can look through can cut you. Yes, I *was* tired. My thoughts were making no sense.

I wasn't only tired. I was angry too. Maggie and I had done growth courses. We believed in equality; we believed in expressing our - Ah, what the hell! What was all that helping us? We were still alienated. We were still talking past each other. There was something we didn't understand. The passions grew. I would become stony, retreat into the cool shadows of a cave-like place within myself. She would ignite. What was it that was happening? Words would fly like arrows; accusations were medieval maces, heavy and spiked. Former insights and pledges would be driven to their knees and good intentions would crumble, falling buildings in a nuclear wind. In the small hours the pillow under my cheek gets hot. I can't sleep. I turn the pillow to the cool side. Slowly, it gets hot. I turn it to the cool side. Dammit. Why can't this woman see reason? But then, again, what about *my* stuff? Because, if you look at …

The bee was silent, myopically examining whatever was keeping it from taking the air and liberating itself into the infinity of the morning. It was directly above my forehead. Quite tricky to keep your eye on what the bee was doing and watch for the slightest change of speed in the car ahead. I did not want to end up standing next to the wreck of a car, dazed blue lights flashing, blocking the busiest highway on the Southern continent … all because of a bee, a bee that can't see, can't sense that the flaming passenger window is wide open. And has been so since I left home, dammit.

The traffic slowed down. I changed lanes, not that that helps on this highway. The fast lane becomes as all lanes are, at this time of day. Glancing out, I saw that the demolition of the old gasworks had progressed considerably since last week. What a satisfying job that must be! Swinging a steel ball into a wall of collapsing bricks. It came to me that that was what Maggie did. She had done it the night before, swung her wrath hard on me. Something had collapsed between us. Did I harbour some sort of envy when she went into her flamenco anger, that demolition mode? Was I too decent, too formal, to admit my own nasty little hurricane buzzing away in the distance. My mode is ice.

She had clutched the glass on the bedside table, an arc of water flaying the duvet, and in rock-splitting rage, smashed it against the wall, pieces bursting - "A-*gain*! You're doing it a-*gain*!" - the impact of splinters shattering on the final word.

I changed lanes. I preferred this route to the one that I'd used previously. Coming in from a new direction as I'd done in the past few months, I'd …

The bee was gone. I stopped at traffic lights. I glanced at the dashboard. It wasn't there. I rolled up the passenger window at last, drove to the check-in of the parking garage, with a funny ironical relief. But there was something else that I felt.

I would 'phone Maggie at her work. I would say, I'm sorry, there's stuff of mine dogging us and I admit my subtle verbal battery. I shall pick up the pieces, try to avoid the splinters sticking into my palm when I caress the carpet, feeling for lost bits. Perhaps we could do it together, drop the shards into a shuttle. You have to be careful of glass. And she smiles at the other end of the 'phone. I know that because I can hear it in the husky emotion, vulnerable but not cringing. She loves me and says so. I feel the same pushing up in me and tell her. And we both pause, wrung by the sadness that our night has been soured by such gall, knowing, at a blind place in us, that there is something neither us understands. But, thank God, the bitterness at least retreats; it melts away, as an unwanted person leaves a gathering.

I drove up the slight slope of the seamed cement ramps through the constant twilight of the parking garage, floor after floor, to the eighth. After the call, if I owned what I needed to own, as easily as she mostly did, Maggie and I would be free again, to be what we could be to each other.

Two weeks later I discovered the bee wedged between the dash-board and the windscreen. It was crisp as a dead leaf.

§§§

Hofmann

Khaki afternoon when I wandered adrift in the dullness of sameness, alone through the house, found myself sitting on the floor of my parents' room dusting the violin case which had lain on top of the cupboard for an oblivion of years. And in it, the violin. Out of tune. Somehow disappointing. Dad had played the violin when he was a young man. I couldn't see him playing the violin now. I lost interest.

I had also seen the canister at the bottom of the cupboard, in amongst Dad's shoes. He had brought it back from the War in North Africa. He showed it to us once. The catch clipped opened and closed neatly and my father spoke with admiration of "this kind of engineering". I found it odd. It had been a German canister, belonging to an Enemy. How could one speak with admiration of anything *they* had made?

Inside the canister which opened and closed with clipped precision, there were two other things: a chess set in a soft muslin bag and a belt which had belonged to a German soldier.

The buckle of the belt seized my scrutiny. The Swastika I knew. I had seen it in films and books. The

Eagle perched on it was something I hadn't seen before. And then the Motto. I understood it, or perhaps, remembered when my dad had spoken about the belt. Three German words. They meant "God with us". How could they say that? I thought. They were the enemy and had done so much wrong.

Inside the belt there was a name: *Hofmann*.

It was written, or rather, scratched in, with a ballpoint or some such pen. The texture of the canvas had made writing the name difficult. You could see that he had struggled.

He.

A man named Hofmann had struggled to write his name into his belt. The thought became increasingly troublesome to me.

He had not wanted anyone to steal his belt. He would feel angry.

He would feel.

He had sat one evening and written his name into his belt, into his helmet, into his shirt, because last week some so-and-so had stolen his gloves. And there was no getting them back. Damn' nuisance. But if someone took his belt, he would be able to find it more easily. Confront the thief and say, This is my belt! There could be no arguments if his name was in it. He could feel a little more secure.

He could feel.

He could feel secure; he could feel anger, indignation, sorrow, happiness, terror, joy, warmth, hatred.

Hofmann.

I felt my eyes burning. Perhaps Dad had taken it off the dead body, pulled it out from under the heavy back. Perhaps he had found it lying around. Yes, perhaps it was lying around. It could be that Hofmann was alive, that he had one day in the War just thrown his belt away, that he had survived. There was no blood on the belt.

A child growing up alone, as I was, has a richer fantasy world, they say. But Hofmann is not a fantasy. All we who have approved war know that, somewhere in our bones.

******

We must have seemed unusual tourists, my wife and I, welcomed at the "Lübecker Camping" entrance by the stocky grey-headed proprietor. It was out of season. Our combi stood alone under the autumn poplars and we reminisced about the Marienkirche over the bratwurst we had bought for supper. Wonderful old Hanseatic city,

Lübeck. The conical Gate towers, Barlach's sculptures. It had been special to stand in the silence of the nave of the cathedral where Marika's father had been christened, a kind of pilgrimage for her in her mid-20s.

I noticed the proprietor ambling around the grounds, then near the combi. It looked as if he wanted to chat, probably had nothing to do.

"Nederland, I see," he said in German, looking at our number-plate. We smiled and Marika once again explained that we were not from the Netherlands. We had only bought the combi there.

He was intrigued by her accent: pre-War, he said, a colonial purity! Marika explained to me and we laughed. We were from South Africa, we said, 12,000 kilometres away.

He pursed his lips thoughtfully and with a kind of growing irony, he said, "I was in Africa. Once. I was there with Herr Rommel". He tossed his head lightly in distant mockery on the last two words.

I found myself gently stroking the canvas texture of the combi seat. He was still speaking, Marika, listening. But I was feeling a pressure or something on my cheekbones, under the skin. Something like that. I can't really say what. A relief, perhaps. I don't know whether he was aware of my feelings. Now, twenty years later, I think of Walt Whitman's poem: touching lightly with the lips, the face of the dead enemy.

I felt then to take his shoulders or face in my hands and speak through tears, say the words of healing, or sorrow, or comfort.

Or simply, as the flood subsided, stretch out my hand, to shake his, and say, "Guten Abend, Hofmann."

§§§

The Sculptor

The buzz at the door made her look up. Against the frosted glass was the dark shape of a head, fragmented at the edges. Some instinct said to her, Don't answer, but it was nonsense: she had been in the new place for more than a month, but her fears were still there. It was, of course, being on her own, smarting from a broken relationship in another province, all that ...She put down the electric plug that she'd been fixing and walked to the door. The safety chain was on. She clicked open the door keeping the chain taut and looked through.

A flush of recognition ...She unchained the door.

"My goodness me," she said, looking at him. It had been ... what, two years, since she'd last seen him. "Come in, come in," she welcomed, stepping aside. He looked quite different with his hair bushier and wearing ordinary clothes.

"I got your address from prison," he said turning to her.

"I thought you might have. It's so good to see you," she said. "Let me look at you."

He turned, facing her directly. He seemed taller, she thought. And still the less-than-handsome looks that she found interesting. What a surprise. His body was fuller and the gauntness about the eyes was gone. She caught herself - at the time of doing work at the prison – she had caught herself thinking, There's something here. Under this man's hardness, the shell that he presents to other prisoners, there was something else. A depth, a likeability. She supposed, as with so many people in his situation, that there had been a momentary madness, something snapping and he had been involved in some violent crime. "I stabbed him with a screwdriver," he'd once told her. She wasn't keen on the details. I'm a delicate sensibility, she had thought with irony. Artists must be sheltered from such horrors. But she did speak to him about it. He was not a long-term prisoner. He would be out in some years. And here he was. Out.

"See you're fixing a plug," he said, to fill the awkward moment.

"Some tea?" she asked. He nodded, still self-conscious, rubbing his elbow, looking about her flat. His eye caught something. She paused. "What?" she asked.

He nodded at the corner of the room. She smiled, going into the kitchenette. It was the sculpture. A sculpted head that he had made over the months when she had coached them. A head of pride and serenity.

58

Surprising, really, she had thought at the time, that a prisoner can create an object radiating such peace. She had become unashamedly attached to it, recognising the talent. And she wasn't alone. After the exhibition of the prisoners' work, Raoul Derwent had written in his column `Art Therapist Strikes Gold with Prisoners' and he made a special mention of this piece of sculpture. In fact, he had offered to buy it and she said no. This was personal. It was something that the prisoners used to express themselves, to find dignity and self-worth. But her own admiration for the piece was enormous. She kept touching it. Now - incredibly - it was part of her life because at the last session she had had with them - lots of cake and tea and laughing – he had presented it to her, his eyes glistening. "Take this," he'd said. "I'll make another one. When I get out."

"I can't," she said. "That's yours. That's part of your … your soul".

"I know," he'd said with a skew smile. "Now it's part of your soul".

At first she had refused and then she sensed the intention and accepted. "When I want to see it," he said, "I'll come and visit you."

She had wondered whether she would ever see him again. Would he ever give his art a second thought once he was free? Did any of the prisoners feel for what they had done in those classes? She had to brush off a creeping melancholy that day as she drove home.

The piece had gone up country with her, been admired rather reluctantly by her lover, even had a seductive price hung on it by an art dealer, but she had refused. I'll never part with that, she thought, not without a certain wistfulness.

"Do you remember that afternoon?" he said, coming into the doorway of the kitchenette.

"Which one?"

"The first afternoon we did sculpture."

"Oh, yes." She smiled. "I told you about Michelangelo, when he made 'The Moses'." She put out the cups on a tray and reached for the packet of biscuits. She took up a knife to open the plastic. He stepped forward. "Let me," he said.

She handed him the packet and the knife, but her hand had brushed his. She turned away looking for teaspoons. It's OK, she said to herself. You've been alone for several months. You're on edge. You did find this man attractive. You admitted that to yourself at the time and dealt with it. But now, the "dealing with it" is swept away. Is this heart of hers starting its nonsense again? Just control it, she says to herself, finding the teaspoons, finding the sugar, pouring the milk into a little jug.

"There you are," he said, emptying the biscuits onto the plate.

He was so different. He was poised and gently strong. The drabness of the prison had been washed from him, from his face and his body. It was all in her imagination, of course. Below the surface he could still be the criminal he had been. But her calm was gone. Some weather in her was turning.

Relieved she noticed him turning away, back into the lounge. That afternoon... The one when she spoke about Michelangelo and The Moses, how the sculptor had worked at it for months, paring away the translucent marble, each little flake, with hands of love and how, when it was done, in all its monumental splendour, he stood back, staring. Staring at what he had done with a strange awe and as the moment grew in him, he had taken up the hammer, picked it up with the force of an angry, anguished father and struck the knee of the figure, shouting "Speak, Damn you!"

She stopped. She'd heard something. His voice in the lounge. Was he talking to himself? She slowly closed a drawer, listening. She switched off the kettle. Then she heard it again.

"You think you're so larny, don't you?"

He sounded angry. Was it anger? She strained to hear.

"Why didn't you tell me ..." There was deep resentment.

She was scared. He had probably found the screwdriver she had been using for the plug. Her heart was lurching.

"Too high and mighty ..."

She thought of the front door. Could she jerk it open quickly enough and run down the fire escape? Her throat was dry. What a mistake she had made to let him in. But how was she to know? She couldn't have known. So he had harboured this resentment for her all that time, all those months that she visited the prison, with her art materials tucked under her arm. He had never said anything to her, never owned what he really felt.

"Too proud ... I've thought about you ... so long ..."

She stared at the tea cups not seeing them, paralysed. Was she being "Polly Paranoia", as her ex-lover had once called her? Perhaps she could reason with him.

She moved out of the kitchenette, letting the edge of the room slowly reveal him. He was standing there with the screwdriver in his hand. He was facing the corner, looking at the sculpture.

Then he was across the room and jabbed it. He stood back. Even before she could catch breath, protest, shout at him, he had stopped. Then she saw for the first time that his body was relaxed.

She took a breath. "What're you doing?" she asked, taken aback, curious, the tension draining from her. It had been a piece of theatre.

"I can't stop thinking about this figure. Like you, it's always been with me." His face was open and thoughtful.

For a moment she didn't want to think about the import of "like you".

"You must have it back," she insisted.

"It speaks to me", he said, as if he hadn't heard.

"Speaks to you?" She caught faint irony in his voice.

"It asks me, Can you do it again?"

She wanted to say something.

"Shh …" he said, playfully lifting his finger to his lips. "If you listen, you'll hear it. It's speaking now."

Her heart pounding had eased. She felt safe. She could risk here. He was as likeable as ever. Her instincts were telling her that he had chosen to heal his wounds, to heal the pain of what he had done. He was rubbing off the stamp of his incarceration. The sense of humour and imagination and self-worth were firmly rooted. And growing. She felt she had been a bit silly.

"What does it say?" she said, drawing near.

"It says, I think you can do it again, even though I had my doubts. I've had to wait all this time to hear it."

"Is that what it's saying to you?" she asked. She felt she was running barefoot over soft grass. Her eyes were brimming.

"Yes," he said, putting the screwdriver down. Then he saw her tears. "Why're you …"

"You know me, I believe in letting it through," she said, going back to the kitchenette. Her eyes itched and she wiped them.

"I've only been painting," he called from the lounge. "No sculpture."

She brought in the tray and set it down. "You've been painting?" Her brow puckered, incredulously.

"Yes. Did quite a lot." He gave a little laugh. "I've even sold one. For quite a lot, I'll have you know."

She regarded him. "You know what?"

"What?"

"I want to see your work. I want to see what you've done."

"Now?"

She nodded.

"But ..." he smiled, "you've just made tea".

"There's more," she said. "There's a lot of tea in that cupboard of mine".

He looked steadily at her for a moment, warmed inside of his smile and then was gone.

She stood looking at the sculpture for moment, walked to it. On the floor she saw a tiny flake. She picked it up and held it in her palm. Precious thing.

§§§

Dust

I am dust. I am the shadow between the sun and the gravel road that has once more become quiet. There are moments when the blue curve of the sun clears and I subside again, satisfied. The sun is bright.

There are flat-topped koppies fringed with rock. They curve finely to the plain. The distant hills are rounded as if by water, a long time ago. Fragments of uprooted sedimentary rock are like pieces of striated woodgrain. This ancient wound is softened by dust. Here is history. When the earth knew only the warm slime, these rocks were old. But I am older. I am dust.

There is a smile in me for the wind has come. It whips me up, lifts me, I swirl, turning my back, my front around and again. Expanding, I skim the earth that races below me. I expand, tall now, again the shadow between sun and hill and striation. I skim the earth with young brown energy, curving my back, my front, my face. I pass through solitary trees, sliced by the blades of windmills that were, a moment ago, turning languidly. Then, slowly, like a sober realisation, the wind drops and I become shoulderless. I settle again.

I am made of a fine stuff. I can filter softly through cracks in boulders. Or settle on the branches of the cypress tree and on the gravestones below. The footpaths have my powder, ready for foot and stick.

At the huts I lie lightly against the daub walls in drifts. There are evening sounds. I listen. An emaciated dog sniffs, haunts the rubbish dump like the dream of the undernourished, trots off lightly, even on air. I lie in drifts. There are no capricious breezes tonight and I so wait. The stars are clear. I am quiet now.

Morning gives to no wind and day fills the plain with light and heat. I am patient. I can wait. In the dry river bed there is a mosaic of cracked mud. I gather in the labyrinth of cracks. Here is a tree. I lie on a thorn.

Mud cracks crumble, mud flakes soften and there is dust. The mosaic disappears. The rock fringed koppies are memory: there was a time when the plain was high, but the horizon sank and the koppies now stand alone. I blow with wind to the hills.

Once, all was water and I gathered on the seabed, disturbed by fish with bird-colours, eels like breezes, currents like wind. If I looked at the underside of the water I saw ripples like cirrus cloud. A tail, a gill flicked me and I was ballet with the sea-weed. And then, I subsided and waited with silent patience. The waters withdrew. My mud was exposed and I became a mosaic.

Now the plains and the sky and far day lie wide open. I hide in the tunnels of the wind. Tumbleweed, paths, rocks accelerate under me. I am drunk with turning. I turn pollen in me in a high spiral and laugh. Pollen is young in colour. It gives life and my footwork is fleet.

Clouds gather. Little by little, bits of water fall. On the earth water flows a brown-red plait. In the susurrus of the riverbed, I sink. I am thick and moving and without sleep. The rain washes memory to me, it washes memory from me, around and again.

I am made of a fine stuff. I am old. It is for the wind that I wait. The huts, the white walled house, the rocks, the stream on the plain - all wash away, blow far. The day lies with open arms. Stars pierce the night sky. Far in the universe small planets turn. They have their plains, their dust, crooked cracks in massive boulders darken like premonition. Dust is a kind of longing. In space meteors fall soundlessly.

Someone wipes me from a plastic sun baked vase. The gravestone is dusted off. Lightly I still lie in the hollows of the carved name, the date. In the distance, dustwind spirals through a barbed wire fence.

§§§

Kassiem, Nazeema and the Devil

Kassiem's wife Nazeema was trafficking with the devil and it was making him the hell in. When he challenged her, she denied it. He had thought about it at work, wiping sawdust from his brow, and thought about it at home. Watched her. Tried various things, like putting out the garlic. He even went to see the imam. But there were still signs. And she would simply pass them off as something else.

Take the night he found tracks below her bedroom window. Clear marks that could only have been made by cloven hooves. She said it was a dog, the Doberman from next door. Kassiem said, How could it get through the fence? She pouted, arguing that it was easy for a dog to do that. Or it could have been a rat, she said. Or a cat. Kassiem pricked up his ears. A black cat? he said, with a trick up his sleeve. Walking right into it she said, Could have been. Aha! Kassiem thought, interlocking his fingers over his paunch. The devil, he expounded with precision, often took the form of a black cat because the devil, being who he was, or what he was, could change his form. The devil could look like anyone or anything. Maybe, she said and went off to make some tea.

Kassiem frowned. It always seemed to end like this. Was she saying, Yes, I see the devil, I traffic with him, I smell the sulphur, I feel the heat of his glare? Or was she innocent? At some point in every argument, he found himself weakening, looking at her lustrous eyes, the smoothness of her golden brown skin, the long black hair hanging deep into her back. She had always been a little mysterious. His friend, Abduragman, also said so. He had spoken to Abduragman when he dropped in after work sometimes. And Abduragman had said, Well, he didn't know about the devil; maybe, maybe not.

Kassiem watched Abduragman talking to Nazeema in the kitchen. Perhaps she would say something to him. But when they brought the tea tray, they would be smiling or even laughing. Kassiem felt irritated as he tried to fish out the tea leaves floating in his tea. Abduragman was a man and a friend, but he didn't seem to understand the seriousness of the matter.

Kassiem tried the garlic again. He bought a large truss and cut the cloves neatly with his kris: thirteen cloves into seven slivers each. That would do it. He put some under her bed when she was not there, some in the lounge under the carpet, some in the garden under her

71

window and some in the back yard. North, South, East and West. Then he said a rite.

But Nazeema became more mysterious than ever. She seemed happy for no reason. Her step was light. She was in a world of her own. There was no change in her, as far as Kassiem could see. Nothing. He became obsessed. When Abduragman came around, he said to Kassiem, It's not anything to worry about: women get like that; they go through phases. Even Abduragman's talking in the kitchen with her didn't help anymore. Perhaps his parents had been right when they said she was too young for him. But it wasn't age, Kassiem thought. It was the devil.

He bought some expensive dates and went to the imam again. Eating the dates as they strolled expansively up the road from the Mosque, the imam quoted something Gandhi had said about the devil, something about the devil within. Kassiem couldn't remember what it was. But it wouldn't be important because Gandhi was a Hindu. And the imam had eaten all his dates in the process. In the dusk below Table Mountain, Kassiem hurried home. It felt to him that the whole world was against him. And the devil was sitting on top of Devil's

Peak laughing his foul, sulphurous breath over the city lights that evening.

He would wait, Kassiem thought to himself, narrowing his eyes. Bide his time. Sooner or later she would give herself enough rope to hang with. Perhaps a trap. He could set a trap for her, but he didn't know yet what it could be.

He decided not to tell Abduragman about his new strategy. He had begun to feel that the man didn't take him seriously. And that was annoying.

So he waited. Nazeema seemed more subdued to him and he would find her staring out of the kitchen window at the cranes in the harbour. Or staring at the flowerbed (where he had seen the cloven imprints). That sort of thing. He felt that something was brewing. Sometimes she was out of the house for a little while and then came back without any groceries. Perhaps that was the key. *That* was the time when she saw the devil.

Now it couldn't have been anywhere near their house, because others would see it too. He would have to follow her.

So it was that one afternoon Nazeema put on some smart clothes and scent (he noticed), and breezed off down the pavement, not seeing that he was a little way behind her. She turned up the cobbled side street with youthful energy, her black hair lifting slightly as she went. Kassiem soon found himself a little out of breath and thought once again, I must lose some weight.

She reached the last of the semi-detached houses and began to walk through the long grass next to the highway. She was heading, he saw, for Devil's Peak. She crossed the highway, not in the least aware of him, but he would have to be careful. If she looked back just once... but she didn't. She began to climb up the slight incline above the highway. He ducked down till she was well above the road. Then he quickly ran across, trying to see where she had gone.

He must not lose her now, he thought. This was going to be the final proof of her trafficking. Appropriately, he thought with a grim smile, it would be exposed on Devil's Peak itself. Never had a mountain been so aptly named.

As he began moving up, he had a creeping uncertainty. The devil had many forms, he knew. Would it take the shape of a goat or a rat or even a djinn, as in the stories of his childhood? He felt fear, tinged with excitement. He, Kassiem, would this very day see the devil and be able to tell the imam and Abduragman and everyone else. But, above all, he would have the evidence he needed to put Nazeema in her place. She wouldn't be able to deny it this time.

Just ahead, she was clambering between two immense boulders and then she disappeared. Oh no, he thought, climbing faster.

He came to the boulders, his heart battering at his ribs. Gingerly, he walked between them and then backed out smartly.

The boulders were a natural gateway to a clearing and Nazeema was standing in the middle of that space.

Kassiem thought quickly. He would climb to the top of boulders and be able to look down.

He struggled up the side of the boulder, lying his cheek on the warm rounded expanse, dragging his belly. At the top he held his gasping breath. He pulled himself to the edge.

Nazeema was still standing there, not aware of anything, elegant and silent in the clearing. Waiting, he thought with a leer. Far below was the hum of cars on the highway.

Again Kassiem felt the pang of fear. Would it be in the form of a djinn? The Scales, the Eyes of Fire, the vast Bat-like Wings? Would he, Kassiem, be able to stand it?

Then Abduragman walked into the clearing and embraced Nazeema.

Kassiem's heart stopped. His eyes burned. Then his heart started up again. He clutched the rock surface. He began to back down, with a growing understanding, slithering over the last part of the surface of the boulder and ran through the grass wildly, wildly towards the highway below.

How brilliant the devil was! What a Prince of Deceit! To take the form of someone familiar rather than some exotic shape from a child's fantasy!

A car skidded to avoid Kassiem, blinded in his triumph, his certainty. Long grass lashed his face. Over the cobbles between the first houses, he ran and ran, all the way home. What a find! What a thing to discover!

He couldn't wait to see Abduragman's face when he told him.

§§§

Mr Lucien and the Cinematograph

If it came to killing, my money was on Mr Lucien. He had a vile temper, unpredictable as quicksilver, and would have been a barbarian had his nature not been refined by a penchant for the beautiful and artistic as a man of the theatre. Despite the storms of his humours, the tether held fast until, on that fateful night, it snapped.

Throughout the months before, we saw the writing on the wall, like Nebuchadnezzar of old. "Take that to Mr Grimmle, Miss Peters," Mr Lucien rasped through teeth, throwing the cloak and the dagger at me. "If he's not satisfied, to the devil with him!"

"But he said …"

With his bald head shining, Mr Lucien put his face close to mine and said, "Mr Grimmle can jump into Table Bay! And inform Miss Pendlebury that I shall not be spending another penny on that costume of hers."

I took the aforesaid properties to Mr Grimmle. With his humour being what it was, Mr Lucien sometimes forgot that I was a woman.

Mr Lucien's humour was becoming more variable. When he was like that, his accent seemed to slip and he sounded more like someone from London than someone from Paris. And I knew the reason for the mind he was in … there had been thirteen empty rows two nights before and the previous night, ten. Patronage at Theatre Royale was not what it had been.

"Well, with 'The Widow's Revenge', " he said, pushing his moustache down again and again, "we shall see a different picture". But he was wrong. On opening night there were five empty rows. A year before we had turned patrons away. What a season that was! "The Mask of the Gypsy". "The Scarlet Daughter Returns". "Mr Renwood's Rapier" What enthusiastic response! With nothing spared on the costumes, names like Mr Baldwyn, Mr Evanesse, Miss Lavinia, and many, many more - the finest players from abroad – graced the stage. And now?

Mr Lucien said, "Bring the glue" and with a brush he put up the posters himself, muttering, muttering. That very morning he had laid off his poster boy.

"It cannot continue in this vein," he said. Was there a tremble in his voice? He packed some of the costumes in a trunk, loaded them onto a carriage and with a wheel-creak it went up the wagon-track to the pawn-brokers in Adderley Street. I had secured the best prices in Cape Town, but it didn't bring Mr Lucien any serenity. Fewer and fewer artistes were applying at the theatre. A month before Mr Lucien himself had to play the heartless landlord in "The Dark Side of the Street".

"It just cannot," he said, shaking his head, staring at the takings one evening. I was staring at him. I was now the stage-manager, fashioner and repairer of costumes, properties manager, the one who switched on the electrical lights for day, the prompt, the one who switched off the electrical lights for night, and I had to cry in the wings like a baby, turn the handle of the wind machine, howl like a blizzard and laugh like a villain. And so, I cannot blame myself for forgetting to do the Approaching Footsteps of the hero in "The Dastardly End of Joshua Nettleton." Mr Lucien was furious, not least because the hero himself, Mr José Machado, had walked out before the final act shouting, "Well, in dat case, I go!" Mr Lucien had to don the hat and cape, run on and discharge the flint-lock. In his confusion he shot the wrong man.

We both knew what the matter was. "Perhaps we should be more modern," I ventured, fearful of upsetting him.

"'Modern'! 'Modern'!" he said, his eyes bright with disdain. "That's all I hear these days, is 'Modern'. Just because we are approaching a new century, we must be *modern*!"

Mr Lucien had stood on the sidewalk, looking past Geraghty's Apothecary, past Mr Aaronson cleaning his nails in the doorway of his tobacconist shop, at that next entrance. There, we both knew, was the garish sign:

THE CINEMATOGRAPH

The Latest Astounding Invention in Photography! The Photo-Electric Sensation of the Day! Wonderful Reproduction of Animated Nature! Every Scene in Motion, Reproduced in Real Life!

And it was there that the patrons streamed in. Sometimes we would see the proprietor, a Mr Maxwell Sheen. He would actually be turning them away at the entrance.

Six months before, Mr Lucien had said, "It's a fad - a novelty just like the Magic Lantern, the kinotograph, the vitascope and zoetrope. By the year Nineteen Hundred and Five no one will even remember the cinematograph. It's just a flickering of pictures," Mr Lucien said, his fingers flickering before his face in mimicry. "Only true art endures."

But that night we had no more than sixteen patrons.

"It is not happening," he said, giving a strange little laugh of disbelief after the show. "It's not happening." He paced up and down the stage as I swept under the seats. "Did you hear about Frank Fillis? Did you?"

I stopped, thought a bit. "That's the circus man in Johannesburg, isn't it?" I said.

"It is. With the creditors at his heels, they had to smuggle him out of the country in one of his own circus baskets."

At that moment we heard someone clearing his throat. We looked over the seats. Out of the shadows stepped Maxwell Sheen. I put the broom down. Mr Lucien came down the stairs.

"I'm begging your pardon," the man said. He gave me a wink. Was it an Irish accent?

When Mr Lucien did not say anything, he said, "I've been awondering, Mr Lucien, we've been neighbours for quite some time now - nine months, I do suppose. Perhaps you and I should consider … well, maybe a partnership. I was awondering …"

He was a rather good-looking man with pencil moustache and black hair neatly parted in the middle. But then I saw Mr Lucien's face. It had turned ugly.

81

"Get this straight, Mr Sheen," Mr Lucien said, his voice quivering. "I am a produceur èn scene artistique. I have no time for the amusements of the riff-raff of this town. Leave my theatre, sir … Go, and never darken my foyer again. DO YOU HEAR?" It sounded as if he wanted to kill.

"I hear very well," said Mr Sheen, evenly. "You know where to find me, should you change the tenor of your thinking, Mr Lucien."

When he had left, I thought that Mr Lucien was going to rip his hair off his scalp. "And don't *you* make eyes at him, do you hear?" he bellowed as he disappeared backstage.

Days passed. Mr Lucien paced the foyer; he paced the stage. I was busy preparing for "Julius Caesar's Last Hour", cutting out the shields, making arm bands, painting gold onto the standards, fitting spearheads onto shafts. Once or twice I saw Mr Sheen passing by, always looking into the foyer, as if he were taking measurements of the place. He smiled at me. I must say, he was rather charming.

Opening night drew near. Baron Wolfgang von Löwenfuss who had been cast in the role of Julius Caesar failed to appear. Someone said they had seen him wearing a pith helmet, boarding the train for the Diamond Fields. Mr Lucien seized the script and began to learn the lines. Between patching the holes in the curtains, fixing the wheel on the chariot and shining up the swords, I tried to help Mr Lucien. He was distracted, losing weight and had dark lines about the eyes. There were no advance bookings.

Opening night came. In the dressing rooms I heard him mutter, "It can't happen." He was clenching his teeth. In the foyer was Mr Aaronson buying a ticket, followed by Mr Geraghty. Apart from them there was no-one else. Up the street, we knew, there was a crowd jostling at the door.

Mr Lucien was pale, flattening his moustache against his face again and again, saying his lines over and over, forgetting them, blaspheming. The other actors wandered about, disgruntled at their wages. At the last minute he said to me, "Brutus hasn't arrived. You'll have to stand in."

"What?" I said. "But I'm a woman".

"Don't question me, curse it! Do as I say. Here's a wig." He seemed asthmatic.

Brutus didn't have many speeches and Calpurnia could prompt line for line. I peeped hurriedly at the script behind the curtain and then I peeped in to the audience.

The two gentlemen sat expectantly in the empty auditorium.

The play started. The wars were fought, declamations made, conquests announced. The curtain got stuck after the third act and had to be torn down. One of the electrical lights blew up, just about giving Mr Lucien heart failure. Between scenes, he was in great turmoil. It was the scene at the Senate. He advanced, forgot words, was prompted by Calpurnia. The Senators advanced. I moved among them. Then, I leapt forward, the dagger up high. "For Rome," Calpurnia prompted from behind the curtain. "For Rome!" I cried. Mr Lucien's face, purple-veined, dissolved in agony as he said, "Et Tu, Bruté". Then I stabbed him.

But he wrested the dagger from my hand, his eyes suddenly bright, the vial of false blood spilling across his toga. He stormed down the steps of the stage, shouting "Juggernaut! Juggernaut!" Up past the bemused pair in the audience he ran and out at the foyer. I shouted "Stop, Mr Lucien!" The whole cast followed after. "Stop him!"

He wasn't in the foyer. The pavement was empty. A wizened old Hottentot man passing by was startled by a street suddenly full of Romans. He waved vaguely and said, "Dat way."

I ran to the third entrance, holding onto my wig, my toga lifting on the night breeze, up the stairs, into an auditorium, in time to see the sea of faces plunged into darkness. A collective moan went up. The light had come from a little aperture in the wall above all the heads. I knew that that was where Mr Lucien must be, at which point a rather ruffled Mr Maxwell Sheen fled past me.

Through the semi-dark I made my way toward the sounds of smashing and bashing of something. On a door it read PROJECTION CHAMBER. The noise ceased.

I entered the room. There in the half light lay Mr Lucien gasping, gasping, one hand clutching at his heart; in the other hand, a broken dagger. All around him were the ruins of what could only have been the cinematograph and curls and curls of black shiny ribbon bleeding from it.

All that happened two years ago. Mr Lucien didn't survive the night. The strain went straight to his head and his heart gave in. Mr Sheen refunded his patrons and when the hospital carriage had creaked off, taking Mr

Lucien away, he turned to me and holding my hand, he said, "Hmm. Such a pity."

I married Maxwell Sheen three months later and we journeyed to the city of Johannesburg where he had a much larger cinematograph imported from New York. I really began to enjoy the motion pictures, but I have often thought, Maybe true art will endure in the theatre, as Mr Lucien said. But those flickering images of the cinematograph … passing fad they may be, but they've got something.

§§§

Return

The office was overwhelming, a storeroom really, with shelves on both sides reaching to the roof, shelf upon shelf of files, books, folders, numbered boxes, loose sheaves of paper, with a handful of books on top of a little ladder and a trestle table sagging under piles of documents, files, more books. Many files were too full and had been tied up with string, dog-eared paper squeezing out here and there. On the floor a stack had spilled amongst the small canyons of bound newspapers.

On the shelves there were bits of cardboard tacked on, each with scrawled lettering - *Ta* to *Tu*, *Va* to *Vu*, *Wa*, *We* - a kind of classification system. On the table too, there were sheets of paper with pencilled lettering. Everything in the office was under a thin layer of dust.

The young man had let himself in and closed the door. He took a deep breath, once again surveying the place. He wondered if the old man was there. It was easy to miss him between the piles. The little table at the door, under a dusty cone-shade, as before, had scattered documents, an ink-pot with a dipping pen, open files, a little vial of dried glue, an ashtray of cigarette ends, a bottle-lid with paper-clips, an earless mug crammed with pencils and pens and a six-inch ruler. In a teacup two or three cigarette-ends lay soaking in some tea.

Above the table was a bulletin board, as always, crowded with memos, drawing-pinned and stapled, some tucked in under others. A few lay on the floor.

The young man heard something. He peered between the piles to the misty window panes. It was the old man. He was busy feeding a stray cat below an open pane … a little milk in a saucer. Nothing's changed, thought the young man with a smile. He wasn't going to risk walking through the precariously-balanced stacks of documents and folders.

He's a little balder, the young man thought. A little greyer about the temples, still wearing the same yellowed shirt and waistcoat and ribbon-tie, almost as if he never takes them off. He's podgier about the middle.

The old man peered back from the window, screwing up his eyes, lifting his chin to see through his bifocals.

"You again?" he said to the young man as he emerged, but was immediately preoccupied.

"Yes, sir," said the young man, full of memories of previous visits. He stood to one side so that the old man could get by to the table.

"You're quick." The bald head ducked under the table, fishing for a tripod. "Here." The young man put it in place and sat down.

The old man himself wiggled his own chair out behind the table and fitted himself into the cramped space. With his elbows leaning on the table, he lit a cigarette, waving the match about, dropping it into the ashtray. "It was just the other day, that you ..." His elbows made room amongst the documents.

"Feels like it," the young man reminisced.

The old man let his eyes run over the bulletin board, exhaling smoke. He made a note on the back of an envelope and stuck it on the board. "So you want another placing..." He licked a finger, paging through a file, reaching for a pencil. It was blunt. Under a document he located a blade.

"Yes, I'd like another placing."

The old man sharpened the pencil. "Where?" The shavings curled into the teacup.

"The Earth," the young man said.

"Again?" The old man was examining the pencil point. Then he wrote in the folder. "Don't understand it." He reached for the little ruler and underlined something. "You can't seem to get done with the place." He closed the folder and slid it onto a pile on the floor. "Well, let's see what we can do for you."

He got up and stood at a shelf, letting his finger run over the files, raising his chin to see through his bifocals. He found what he was looking for, drew it out and opened it.

"Yes..." he said, coming back to the table, "fairly recent ..." He paged through, reading here and there. "Yes, I remember ... This is impressive, this one. You've been around. Dum-ti-dum-ti-dum. You want the same again?"

The young man became earnest. "No, I want something new."

"Nothing new under the sun, my man.

The young man smiled. "I know."

"Something different... new... there are possibilities..." The old man leaned over backwards, reaching for a thick volume behind him on the shelf, he lay it before him, biting his lower lip as he paged. He tapped his cigarette in the teacup.

"Asia?"

"No, I know Asia well."

The old man pulled a face. "I see ... Hmm, you've got Prehistory to your credit ... Australopithecus, Homo

Habilis, Neanderthal … Then again Aztec, Maya, Inca. Even Easter Island. Not many who can say that. But something new, you say …" He paged on in the thick book.

The young leaned forward. "Twentieth-century … Early twenty-first … Do you have anything in that line …"

"Twen…ty…first…cen…tury… Oh yes. Look, you've got great potential there." He flicked back a page or two. "What part do you want?"

"I don't mind."

The old man let his finger-nail run down a column. "America - North - America - South - I can offer you both." He disappeared for a moment in the cigarette smoke.

"No … Not 'North'. It's too … um … established."

"Europe … I don't suppose …"

"No, I've been there."

"'Been there; Done that'," said the old man without humour. "Probably followed the old path, hey? - Egypt, Greece, Rome, Gaul -"

"Yes," said the young man, smiling at the memory.

"What about Africa?" He was paging again.

The young man thought a little. "Mm … Africa … Sounds good."

"Ivory Coast? East Africa? Oh no, you've been in East Africa … that prehistoric thing again …"

"Yes." For a moment the young man's mind sped back over the millennia. "It was the Afar Triangle... four million years ago..."

"That's quite a bit. Zanzibar?"

"No, I don't feel strongly feel strongly about Zanzibar. A placing must feel right, you know. It should seize my imagination … I don't just want …"

"I wouldn't know," said the old man, crushing his cigarette. "I've never had a placing … Now how about the South? What does that sound like?"

"The South of Africa?"

The old man nodded, fitting another cigarette to his lips. Coughed a bit. "Let's look at the combination." He struck a match and lit it. "Late-Twentieth century, the South of Africa … You wouldn't prefer the time of, say... the pioneers? Or perhaps later … the middle of the Twenty-first century, more established … something like that?"

"No," said the young man, "it sounds right … Southern point of Africa. Early twenty-first, as I said."

"Good." The old man gave a routine sigh. He drew the file out from under the thick volume and paged about in it. He found a page. "What do you want to be? Male or female?"

"Man. Male."

"Male..." The old man ticked a block. "Brothers and sisters?"

"Yes."

"Combination?"

"Any combination, I don't mind."

The old man ticked. "Theme?" He rolled the cigarette ash off on the edge of the cup.

The young man hesitated.

"Last time you chose blood 'n guts ..." The old man peeped at a previous page.

"I know." The young man became thoughtful.

"Did you learn something... last time?"

"I don't know."

"It's always difficult..." The old man was tapping his cigarette, scratching his stubbled chin with a thumbnail.

"Humaneness ... Um ... Compassion ..." The young man was search for the word. "Er ... I think I'll try that this time."

"Bit vague," said the old man, pulling a face at the page. "Do you want to give it or take it?"

"Um … Both, I think … Give and Take …"

"Got that." The old man ticked a block and made a note next to it.

"Victim or Oppressor?"

"What is the difference … between the two … in this region?"

"Not much … constant somersaulting …"

"What do they learn … with each placing?"

"Some learn. There are some who just like the experience. You can choose. The other day I had a chap in … Well, he's been both … a number of times … Seems to be on the increase, this swopping of roles."

"Could I leave it open?"

The old man pursed his lips. "Well, I don't know. I suppose you could choose when you arrive..." He turned the page.

"Well, then..." The young man seemed ready to get up.

"Um … there's something else …"

"Something else?" The young man frowned.

The old man drew deeply on the cigarette, inhaled and blew out a cone of smoke.

"U-huh. With this region, at this time of history …"

"What?"

"Skin colour … What skin colour do you want to be?"

"Can't I leave that open?" He was impatient to go.

"No, my good man. This one you have to choose now."

The young man winced. He gazed about the office which hung high and heavily over him. His finger traced through the dust on a shelf at his side. Then, the first spark of excitement darted through him, as it always does at the moment of birth.

He took a breath. "OK." Then he told the old man.

The old man made a note. "Interesting choice," he mused. He closed the file and, leaning back, he replaced the thick volume on the shelf behind him. "That's it. Till next time," he said.

The young man pushed the tripod under the table, shook hands briefly, opened the door and went out.

The old man was left behind amid the smoke of his cigarette.

§§§

The Paper Boat

She had been there as a child, a beautiful park with ponds and the greenest of lawns, not overly manicured, stretching through clusters of fir trees down to the Lake. The mountains rising from the far side, out of the waterline, were bulks of hazy dark blue.

She watched him coming through the trees. As always, he had given up time to be with her. She never saw him during the week and they had had some differences on the matter. When he had tried to explain about the deadlines with his promoter, about thematic divisions when you write a thesis, she had laughed at first.

"I'm a country girl," she said, stopping him.

"Country *woman*," he corrected her because he was a feminist. Language, he explained to her, has an insidious way of defining our attitudes. When it came to words, he was precise.

He gave her a peck and they sat down at the edge of a pond floated with lily-pads and lotus leaves, palettes of light green on the dark. The strollers and sitting families had a Sunday serenity about them. Children ran between the trees and she saw a collie chasing a frisbee.

Someone had left a newspaper on the grass and he idly picked it up, glancing at the headlines. She felt the distance hardening between them once more. Why was it so difficult for him to chat to her? Just to say things? Just to be? Was he still at his apartment, eyes glued to the computer screen, while his body lounged at the pond? Would he ever be different? Am I clingy? She had asked herself many times, not without agony. She had recently become aware of how her mind was alive with a traffic of insecurity when she was with him, or, at best, in a mist of dim unease.

He turned to the second page, his eyes now scouring the print. Resisting a sigh, she picked up the Classified Smalls section and pulled off a double page and for no reason began folding it, in half, in half again, turning one of the corners in. She was making a paper boat, as she had done as a child. He muttered something about the government, something he was reading, but she hardly heard him. Tuck in, fold out, this one like this and then that one, also outward. Quite a complicated pattern, now that she thought of it, but she managed when she was little and she was managing now, working as though blind, by instinct, folding, tucking.

"How's your week been?" he said, looking at page three.

The little front prow, the little back prow … and it was quite an art to push out the middle bit, the peaked "mast", so that it was higher than the rims. She looked at it. Perfect. And it was surprising, because she had not made one for what … fifteen, seventeen years? It would float. She leaned over and placed it on the surface of the water.

He lowered the newspaper and looked at her.

She poked at the little boat with her finger. She stared at it on the water and heard her own voice. "It's finished."

He regarded her more closely and then set the newspaper aside. "What's finished?" he asked, shooting a glance at her creation.

When she spoke again, her voice was more steady, even resonant. "It's finished." She might have added "the boat" but something stopped her. It was in her mouth, waiting to be spoken. She said it. "You and me." The little boat was bobbing in a circle, hat-like. A fat yellow fish loomed out of the green water.

He blinked twice. He was a lecturer in Communications. He knew about the dynamics of the impasse - between individuals, factions and nations. His thesis was to be on the psycho-history of something or other, he had told her. And once, when they had fought and she had said, "Be with me … your body and your mind" he smiled and told her how her mind was in fact working at that point. She had listened and then gone home, not knowing quite what it was that crawled with little legs over her thoughts.

He moved his jaw this way and that, thinking, then shifted across the grass, nearer to her, sensing her mood. Had he picked up on her tone? Had he heard what she had said?

He looked at the paper boat and pouted, seeing the potential of illustrating a point. He chose his moment and offered, "It'll sink."

"Oh, I don't know," she said - a gentle, definite counter. He must have heard.

On the side of the boat, the way she'd folded it, she could see part of the word "Smalls". She would rather have the headlines, she felt. She prodded the prow and the boat turned a circle on the water, bobbing. She could see the beginnings of grey seepage moving through the newsprint.

"Paper absorbs water," he said with mock-profundity, a faint smile tugging at his eyes. Then he added, "Especially newspaper" like a father, generous enough to impart his own long-established wisdom.

"True," she said, confident enough to admit it, but grey doubt was beginning to seep into her. "But," she heard her voice say again, "it may be more resistant than you think." And she believed that. She wanted to believe that. Why was she wavering?

Some ducks glided past and ripples took the boat, sideways, beyond her fingers. For a swift second, she grasped after it, her fingers raking air. She felt the pang of some nameless emotion, a loss of some kind. A door closing. A wind dying.

There must have been a current in the pond because the boat moved off, past the lily-pads, to the other side of the pond. But she kept watching it bob, as if she were egging it on, as if there were hopes pinned on it, a doughty little boat, with its points of newsprint. It wasn't sinking.

Don't go down, little boat, keep straight up. If you lean … If you lean, you'll absorb water sooner, and you're not going to do that, stay up, if you can do that …

Any minute now he would begin telling her about facing things, about honesty, about whatever. She turned from watching the boat and looked at him. He was regarding her, as if she were a curiosity, his eyes warm with knowing. This time he would probably throw in what the paper boat stood for in her mind, pinning the thoughts as if they were wriggling insects.

But she rose, tall and silent above him, her eyes never leaving his. She saw the knowing suddenly stealing from his eyes. A realisation of some kind was dropping through him like lead. She was surveying not only his face, but the time it had meant, their time, their lost years. In seconds she relived the endless stretches of quiet frustration, her hope short-circuiting, time and time over. He was contained, this man; he needed little else outside of his world. Or if he did need something - did need her, in fact - was blissfully unaware of it. But to tango, the saying goes, takes two. And she had allowed herself to be led in these choices, to be led to this park, like a child. The gathering storm in her told her that she could no longer lean and sink back into this life. What was on her face now might have been a sad smile were it not for the pain.

He had always been ready with words, comforting her out of what she was really feeling. Now he had no words. The fierce winds in her steady gaze had scattered his words. She turned, walked across the lawns, slowly at first, deliberately, feeling faint resistance from the thick lawns, down the slope towards the Lake.

At the quayside children scampered ahead of the parents who carried Sunday picnic baskets. Their noise scattered her feelings a little. Over the Lake the mountains were vast. She walked along the jetty towards the sound of a petrol engine sput-sputtering in the water. It was the Lake ferry-boat.

She stepped onto it amidst a flurry of excited children and was awash in memory. It was still the same old-fashioned ferry she remembered when her parents had first brought her here. A solid wooden structure, dark and heavy-beamed, muffling the stamp of children's shoes.

The last of the passengers crowded onto it, hemmed in by safety-rails and a man with a grey-black beard in a sailor's cap gave a call. The ferry slowly veered away from the tyres it was moored against, the vibrations of the engine coming through the wood, the mountains drawing her in a strange way, a breeze touching her face, the sky towering beyond the line of summits.

She kept her eyes on the far shore until she was there.

§§§

Ady

I've got a friend. Her name is Ady. She lives in the lemon tree in our backyard. You can't see her. Only I can see her. She's in the branches and you must talk nicely to her, softly, otherwise she can't hear you. Whisper. And you have to be alone. She doesn't come out when there are other people.

When my sister Joanie once looked out of the window and asked, "Who are you talking to, Nina?" I said, "Nobody" and pretended to be scratching the bark of the tree. Other people won't understand Ady. I always have to be alone with her and I have to make sure that the kitchen door is closed because maybe my mother will come and look while I'm talking to Ady.

Ady hears everything I tell her.

That time at school when Miss Crosby shouted at me, when I hid Sipho's apple… I was so cross and when I came home I went straight to the backyard. I knew Ady would be there. Joanie's bedroom window was closed because she was still at school, the high school, they have to stay longer. The kitchen door was closed.

Ady, Ady, are you there?

You have to listen carefully, between the branches. She doesn't always speak. You have to start. Ady, Miss Crosby shouted at me today and I gave Sipho's apple back to him. She said I stole it. I was just playing. I tease Sipho because sometimes he teases me. And, Ady, I don't want to go back to school tomorrow, because Miss Crosby... when she walks in that door she looks like a storm. She's old. Her face gets all creased when she gets cross. She's got white hair... it hangs over her forehead. I'm scared of her, Ady. But maybe she isn't so bad. Once when I played wall-wall, I won and she was standing there and she clapped. Ady, you must be good and I must go and clean my shoes for tomorrow.

It always feels nice when I talk to Ady.

One day when I come back from school there is a big lorry in front of the house next door. Some men are busy carrying furniture out of the house. The lady next door is standing there and looking at boxes full of stuff. They're moving, my mother says. Later on, the lorry is gone and the house is closed up. The neighbours and their little dog which was always barking are gone. The windows in front are big and empty.

On Saturday morning I see a car full of people stopping there. They get out and go into the house. I see them walking around the house and looking at the gutters on the roof. They look at the backyard. There is a girl with them. The next week they move in.

The girl I saw comes to our school now. I wonder if she could be a friend.

In the afternoons we start walking home together. She's got lovely frizzy hair and dark eyes and we talk through the fence in the backyard. She's funny and she makes me laugh. We scandal about Miss Crosby at break and how ugly she is. Well, not always ugly, because sometimes Miss Crosby is nice. My new friend's name is Ayanda. Her mother works and she hasn't got a father.

On Saturday mornings I'm up early and I meet Ayanda at the fence. We talk and then she comes over. We play hospital-hospital. She brings her dolls which are really pretty and they are the patients. I get cross with Ayanda because *she* always wants to be the doctor and she says there can be only *one* doctor. Her grandpa was in hospital and she knows all about it. I have to be the nurse. And I don't want to be. I want to be the doctor who listens with a thing around her neck to people's hearts. Ayanda isn't playing nicely and she goes home.

Sunday afternoon everybody is sleeping. I stand at the backdoor. I walk to the lemon tree.

Ady, Ady, are you there?

I listen. Ady, I'm cross with Ayanda. You know, she's the girl next door. She just wants to be the doctor all the time and I have to be the nurse. Why can't there be *two* doctors? She says that's how it is in hospitals. Now, Ady, I like Ayanda, but what must I do? Must I be the nurse for a while, when we play again? Perhaps I must. Maybe I can be the doctor later, if she gets sick, or something. Do doctors get sick, Ady? Well, I won't get sick if I'm the doctor. Thank you, Ady. You always give me such good advice.

On Monday Ayanda and I play again. She tells me that when they left the other house she had to leave her friend behind. Her friend lives in the attic, above all the rooms. You can't see her. Only Ayanda could see her and nobody knows about it.

I tell Ayanda about Ady. I show her the lemon tree, but we don't go and talk to Ady. Ayanda now tells me that I am her friend. We are best friends. She doesn't want her friend in the attic anymore and a friend that no one knows about. I think about it when Ayanda has gone home again. Maybe I have to say good-bye to Ady as well. That won't be easy.

Ayanda and I go to the beach and one afternoon her mother takes us to the movies. We play and laugh each afternoon and we solved the doctor problem: we now take turns at playing the doctor. The patients appreciate that too. They get healthy more quickly. We also play school-school and I'm Miss Crosby.

One holiday Ayanda and her mother go away and I stand at the fence and look where we played. I know that Ayanda will come back soon. The days pass.

I go to the lemon tree.

Ady, Ady, are you there?

Ady, tomorrow or the next day Ayanda and her mother will be coming back and I won't be able to talk to you anymore. She wants us to be best friends and I won't be able to be friends with you anymore. I feel... I feel funny about it. Inside. It hurts me. Nobody will understand, because they don't know you, Ady. So, I'm saying good-bye. You have always been such a good friend to me. You always gave me advice.

I hope you're not cross with me. I'll always love you.

Ayanda and her mother come back and we go to the circus. It is wonderful. At the end of the year we have a class party with Miss Crosby. She is so funny and we all get balloons. Ayanda's uncle builds a puppet theatre for us in her backyard and some friends come and do puppet shows for us. Afterwards Ayanda and I make our own puppets. My sister Joanie helps us. I am so happy with Ayanda. She will always be my best friend.

But each time, when they go away for weekends, I look at the lemon tree. Sometimes I stand there, but I don't know if I can talk to her, with Ady, I mean. Not after what I said to her, because Ayanda is my best friend now.

I still love you, Ady. But maybe you don't believe that anymore.

Ady, Ady, are you there?

§§§

Other Publications by Will van der Walt

Fifty by Fifty

Fifty flash sagas each consisting of fifty word with wonderful illustrations by the author.

Available on Amazon Kindle

How to Play the Sand

Sand play is a tried-and-tested way of navigating the inner life and supporting helping relationships. As a method it is gentle, creative and incisive.

Available on Amazon Kindle

Prometheus 999

Stories of humour and pathos, oblique and domestic, local and universal.

Available on Amazon Kindle

Stories for Healing

This is a treasury of stories which may be used in a variety of therapeutic circumstances.

Available on Amazon Kindle

§§§

www.ingramcontent.com/pod-product-compliance
Lightning Source LLC
Chambersburg PA
CBHW031843170626
46807CB00004B/1590